An I Can Re[ad Book]

DINOSAUR HUNTER

story by Elaine Marie Alphin
pictures by Don Bolognese

HarperCollins*Publishers*

To Art,
who loves the stories the bones tell
as much as I do
—E.A.

HarperCollins®, ▦®, and I Can Read Book® are
trademarks of HarperCollins Publishers Inc.

Dinosaur Hunter
Text copyright © 2003 by Elaine Marie Alphin
Illustrations copyright © 2003 by Don Bolognese
Printed in China. All rights reserved.
For information address HarperCollins Children's Books, a division of
HarperCollins Publishers, 10 East 53rd Street, New York, NY 10022.
www.harperchildrens.com

Library of Congress Cataloging-in-Publication Data
Alphin, Elaine Marie.
    Dinosaur Hunter / by Elaine Marie Alphin ; illustrated by Don
Bolognese.
        p.   cm. (I Can Read)
    Summary: In Wyoming in the 1880s, a young boy fulfills his dream
of finding a dinosaur skeleton on his father's ranch, outwits a man
who would cheat him, and sells his find to a team of fossil hunters.
    ISBN 0-06-028303-3 — ISBN 0-06-028304-1 (lib. bdg.)
    ISBN 0-06-444256-X (pbk.)
    [1. Fossils—Fiction. 2. Dinosaurs—Fiction. 3. Ranch life—
Wyoming—Fiction. 4. Wyoming—History—19th century—Fiction.]
I. Bolognese, Don, ill. II. Title. III. I can read book.
PZ7.A4625 Di 2003   2002152281
[Fic]—dc21   CIP
                                                                     AC

❖
13 SCP 10

CONTENTS

CHAPTER ONE

After the Storm 4

CHAPTER TWO

Real Fossil Bones? 14

CHAPTER THREE

Something in the Dirt 20

CHAPTER FOUR

A Warning 26

CHAPTER FIVE

The Tricky Stranger 30

CHAPTER SIX

A Real Dinosaur Hunter 39

After the Storm

Wyoming, the 1880s

Ned finished his breakfast. "I'm sure that storm last night washed out some fossils," he said. "I bet I find a dinosaur today!"

Pa said, "Today's a day for work. I need you to check the fences in the south and west fields for storm damage."

Ned followed Pa to the barn. He asked, "Remember when Mr. Granger sold his shells to those fossil hunters? He found those shells on his ranch, and it's right next to ours!"

"Mr. Granger will be checking his fences today," said Pa. "Remember, Ned, ranch work comes before games."

"But fossil hunting isn't a game," Ned said, "not to those fossil hunters. They make their living looking for bones."

Pa said, "You sure do look hard enough, mostly when you should be doing your chores." He shook his head. "Remember that coyote skeleton you found? You were so sure it was dinosaur bones!"

"That was last year," said Ned. "What if I find a dinosaur like fossil hunters want for their museums? Wouldn't that be something? I'm sure I will find one!"

"*After* you check the fences," Pa said. Then he smiled and added, "It sure would be something if you did find a dinosaur."

Ned watched Pa ride off to check on the cattle. "I bet I can check the fences and look for dinosaur bones at the same time," he said.

Ned walked along the ranch fences in the west field. He looked for breaks in the line and fallen poles. The storm winds had blown small rocks around, and mud was drying in the hot sun.

Just then, Ned saw a boy walking across the field.

"Hello," the boy called. "My name's George Sternberg. This your ranch?"

"My pa's ranch," said Ned.

George grinned. "Permission to explore?" he asked, bowing like a grand gentleman.

Ned grinned back. "Sure," he said. "What are you looking for?"

"Fossil bones—big ones," said George.

"Dinosaur bones?" Ned asked. "That's what I'm looking for!"

"Great! Let's look together," said George.

CHAPTER TWO

Real Fossil Bones?

"I haven't seen you around here before," said Ned. "Are you visiting family?"

George said, "My father and I travel together looking for dinosaur bones for museums."

"That's what I want to do!" Ned said. "I want to find a dinosaur and have it in a museum." He kicked at the dirt. "But I haven't found any good fossils yet, just a few shells."

George said, "My father says you have to look real hard. It's easy to miss fossils."

"But dinosaur bones are big," said Ned. "You can't miss them."

"The bones could be buried," George said. "Only a little piece might show."

Ned looked around carefully. He had never been so far out in the west field before.

Suddenly he saw some strange bumps sticking out of a slope.

"Hey, George!" Ned cried. "Look at that!"

The boys ran over. George brushed away the dirt. Then he shook his head. "Just cattle bones," he said. "Dinosaur bones have been in the ground so long, they have turned to stone. These bones aren't stone yet."

"If they were real dinosaur bones, I'd be a real dinosaur hunter, like you and your pa," said Ned.

"Looking hard makes you a dinosaur hunter already," George said. "Most of the time we look hard but don't find anything."

CHAPTER THREE

Something in the Dirt

"I wish I could keep looking for fossils, but I've got to get back to checking the fences," Ned said. "You can look in the south field if you want."

"Thanks," said George.

Ned slid down the slope. He didn't see any breaks in the fence. All the poles were in place. He looked back at George and wondered if he had found any fossils yet. "Dumb old fences," Ned muttered.

Then Ned saw odd shapes in the dirt near the fence. Quickly he got off his horse and knelt down. He brushed them gently, the way George had. They felt like stone, but they looked like bones. And they were big.

"George," he yelled. "Come quick!"

George hurried over. "Wow!" he said. "That looks like a whole skeleton. It's a triceratops! The scientists will want this one for sure! Could we buy it?"

"That would be great!" said Ned. "I'll ask my pa about it as soon as he gets back from checking the herd. Where are you staying?"

"Our camp is by the cottonwoods at the creek," said George.

"We will come tonight!" said Ned.

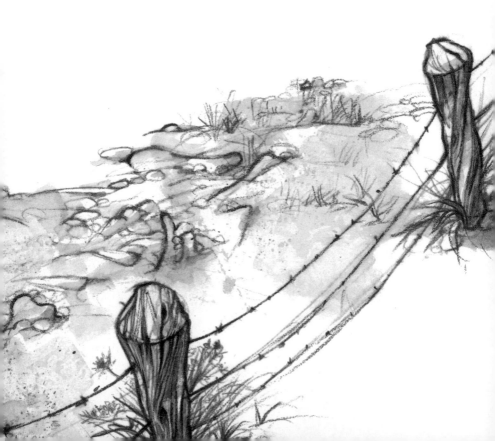

CHAPTER FOUR
A Warning

Ned kept checking the southern fence line, but he did not pay much attention to the fence. He was busy imagining crowds of people looking at his dinosaur in a big museum. He didn't even hear Mr. Granger ride up on the other side of the fence.

"What are you doing way out here, Ned?" Mr. Granger asked.

"I'm checking the fences," said Ned. "But I found a dinosaur skeleton, too!"

Mr. Granger smiled. "Dinosaur bones?" he asked. "Sure it isn't just another coyote?"

Ned blushed and said, "They really are dinosaur bones this time. And a dinosaur hunter will dig them up and put them in a museum."

"Well, maybe," Mr. Granger said. "But be careful. Those dinosaur hunters are tricky!"

"What do you mean?" Ned asked.

"Remember my shells?" Mr. Granger asked. "The fossil hunter who bought them said they weren't worth much. Later,

another fossil hunter offered me more money for them—a lot more. That first fellow had tricked me! I hear they do stuff like that all the time."

"Really?" Ned asked.

Mr. Granger said, "Just be careful dealing with any fossil hunters." He waved and returned to checking his own fences.

CHAPTER FIVE

The Tricky Stranger

Ned checked fences all the way back to the barn, thinking about what Mr. Granger had said. He wished Pa were home.

Ned did chores while he waited for Pa. Suddenly, he heard a horse and a man called out,

"Hello! Are you the boy who found the bones?"

"That's me!" said Ned. "Did George tell you?"

"George?" asked the man. "Yeah, sure, I know George. I hear you found a whole skeleton. My name is Mr. Reed."

"Are you a real live dinosaur hunter?" Ned asked. "I have been looking for dinosaur bones for years!"

"Can I see the bones?" Mr. Reed asked.

"I have to talk to my pa about selling them," said Ned.

"Bones aren't worth much," said Mr. Reed. "But they will trip up your cattle. I will take a look at them—maybe I can clear them away for you for free."

"I thought fossil hunters paid for bones," Ned said slowly. He remembered Mr. Granger's warning. "You'd better meet Pa and talk to him," he said.

Mr. Reed leaned close to Ned. "Tell you what," he said. "I'll give you a silver dollar if you show me those bones now."

A silver dollar was a lot of money, but not for a whole dinosaur! Now Ned was sure this man wanted to trick him.

Mr. Reed said, "If you aren't interested, maybe I will just look around on my own and keep this silver dollar."

What if Mr. Reed found the bones and tried to take them? Suddenly Ned got an idea. "I can show you," he said, "but I can't take your money unless Pa says it's all right."

Mr. Reed smiled.

Ned took Mr. Reed to the west field,
walking slowly. He led Mr. Reed down
some gullies and back out again. Mr. Reed
was sweating. "Are we almost to the bones
yet?" he asked.

At last Ned stopped by the first set of
bones he had found that day. "There it is!"
he said. "My dinosaur!"

Mr. Reed wiped the sweat off his face
and looked at the bones.

"These are just cattle bones!" Mr. Reed said. "You have wasted my whole day. You couldn't find a dinosaur bone if one fell on your head!"

Mr. Reed got back on his horse and rode off toward town.

CHAPTER SIX

A Real Dinosaur Hunter

Ned hurried home. He pumped water so that Pa could wash quickly when he got home. Then he pumped extra water and washed his own face and neck.

At last Ned saw Pa coming. Ned ran to meet him. "Pa!" he cried. "I did it. I found a dinosaur!"

"A real dinosaur?" Pa asked. "You found one? Are you sure?"

"I was checking the fences, and there it was, in the south field," said Ned.

He told Pa about the bones and George while Pa washed up. Then Ned told Pa about Mr. Reed.

"Mr. Reed wanted to trick me," said Ned. "But I tricked him instead. I showed him the cattle bones I found!"

Pa laughed. "Sounds like Mr. Reed met his match when he met you. Now let's go see about this George fellow."

When Ned and Pa reached the dinosaur hunters' camp, Ned called, "Hello!"

"Hi, Ned," said George. "This is my father, Mr. Sternberg."

Mr. Sternberg said, "I'm glad you came. We were about to come find you."

George said, "We had a spy in camp!"

"A spy?" asked Ned.

"He lied to my father," said George. "He really worked for another fossil hunter—Mr. Reed."

"Mr. Reed?" Ned asked. He grinned. "He came looking for my dinosaur, but I showed him the cattle bones instead."

Mr. Sternberg laughed. "Quick thinking, Ned! But we had better get to work before he comes back. I'd still like to buy your triceratops, if you and your pa want to sell."

Ned asked, "Will you put the triceratops in a museum?"

Mr. Sternberg nodded. George said, "They'll even put up a sign that says you found the dinosaur—with your name on it and everything!"

"Just think, Ned," said Pa proudly, "your triceratops!"

"Wow," said Ned. Then he added, "Maybe one day I can join your team of dinosaur hunters for real, Mr. Sternberg!"

Mr. Sternberg smiled and said, "Ned, you already have."

TRICERATOPS
FOUND BY NED CHAPMAN, WYOMING

Author's Note

As pioneers traveled west in the mid-1800s, many of them settled on the open ranges of Wyoming and Montana. Rainstorms and driving winds scoured the countryside, constantly sweeping away the surface soil, and settlers were surprised to discover huge, bone-shaped blocks of stone embedded in their land. Scientists called paleontologists had begun studying fossil remains of dinosaurs in the 1820s, and these new finds out west excited two paleontologists in particular—Edward Drinker Cope and Othniel C. Marsh.

In the 1870s and 1880s, Cope and Marsh paid fossil collectors to hunt for dinosaur bones, and to buy them from western landowners. Each paleontologist wanted to find more fossils and build a better reputation than the other. Marsh worked with Yale University and had better funding than Cope, who was an independent scholar. W. H. Reed collected fossils for Marsh, while Charles Sternberg worked for Cope. Reed and Sternberg often spied on each other so they could be the first to claim a skeleton like the triceratops Ned finds in this story.

Charles Sternberg was famous for the new methods he developed for preparing and transporting fossils. He brought each of his sons into the field with him as soon as they were old enough to help him. George found his first fossil when he was nine, and grew up to become even more skilled than his father at field preparation of fossils. Sternberg was delighted to think that, long after he died, "Those animals of other days will give joy and pleasure to generations yet unborn." He was right.